Nancy Krulik and Ama...

Project Droid

Science No Fair!

Illustrated by Mike Moran

SCHOLASTIC INC.

ISBN 978-1-338-18556-0

12 11 10 9 8 7 6 5 4 3 2   17 18 19 20 21 22

Printed in the U.S.A.   40

First Scholastic printing, February 2017

Cover illustration by Mike Moran
Cover design by Georgia Morrissey
Interior design by Joshua Barnaby

For Danny and Ian, the other half of the bunch

—NK

For Jone, Aura, Anya, Nadine, Alex, Lexi, and Sasha,

my other halves

—AB

To my Project Boys, Patrick and Matthew

—MM

CONTENTS

1.

Surprise!

"Logan! I've got a surprise for you!"

I heard my mom calling. But I didn't move. My mom is an inventor. There's *always* some sort of surprise in her lab.

I was busy fishing the green loops out of my cereal. I wanted to find out if each color really tasted different. But before I could swallow a spoonful, Mom ran into the kitchen.

"Logan!" she said, as she pushed her goggles up onto her forehead. "Didn't you hear me?"

I nodded. "I was going to come as soon as I finished breakfast."

"But this is the biggest surprise yet," Mom insisted.

Mom always says that. So it wasn't very surprising.

"What is it you want most in the whole world?" She smiled.

"That giant box with the trap door? The one magicians use to make people disappear?"

I dropped the spoon. Green cereal
loops and milk splattered all over the
floor.

"Did you get me one?" Now I was
getting excited.

Mom shook her head.

Oh, bummer.

I went back to fishing green loops
out of my bowl.

"This is bigger."
Mom grinned.

Bigger than the
most amazing magic
trick in the whole
world? No way.

"Come on," Mom

said. "You've been asking for this since you were little."

"The only other thing I ever wanted was a little brother."

Mom smiled really wide.

I hopped out of the chair.

"A brother?" I shouted. "You adopted a brother for me?"

"Not exactly," Mom said slowly, "but—"

I didn't hear the rest of what she said. I was too busy running for the garage. That's where my mom has her lab.

But when I got there, I didn't see a baby anywhere.

There wasn't a crib.

Or a stroller.

Or even a diaper.

I peeked under the table. And up on the shelves.

But all I saw were pieces of some of my mom's old inventions: wires, bolts, wheels, and a full-sized plastic skeleton with a top hat on his head. But no baby.

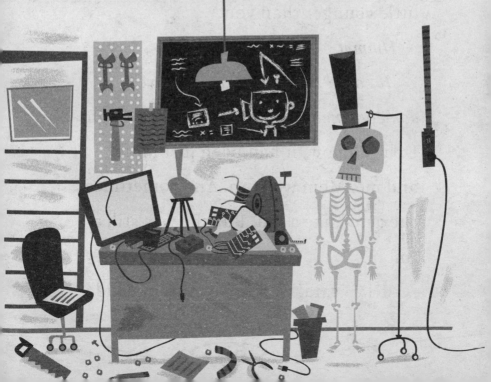

I turned to go back in the house.

That's when I saw *the kid*.

He was standing beneath a chalkboard covered with numbers and weird signs. And he was staring at me.

"That's not a baby," I said.

"No," my mom agreed. "He's just a little younger than you."

Hmmm.

It could be kind of fun to have someone near my age around, I thought. Up until now, it had been just Mom and me. Mom was fun. And sometimes she acted like a kid. But she was still a "mom."

"Hi," I said, walking over to the kid.

"I'm Logan."

The kid just stared at me.

Maybe he was shy.

"What's your name?" I asked him.

The kid still didn't answer. He didn't even move.

"Give him a few minutes," Mom said. "He's still charging."

2.

Can You Keep a Secret?

Just then, the kid blinked. Twice. He scratched his head and yawned.

"Oh, good. Java's all charged up," Mom said.

"Java?" I asked.

"That's his nickname," Mom explained. "It stands for Jacob Alexander Victor Applebaum."

Applebaum. That was my last name.

Which could only mean one thing.

"You built me a robot brother?" I asked Mom nervously.

"Of course not," Mom said.

Phew.

"I built you a robot *cousin!*"

I thought about that for a second.

Maybe this wouldn't be too bad.

"Can he play soccer with me?" I asked.

Mom nodded.

"How about magic tricks?" I asked. "Could he be my assistant?"

"I can program him to do that," Mom said. She snapped her fingers. "Abracadabra. He can do anything a kid can do. Even homework."

"Homework?" I asked. "What kind of homework could a robot have?"

"Whatever homework *you* have," Mom said. "He's going to be in your class at school. It's all arranged."

"You want me to bring a robot to school?"

"Yes," Mom told me. "Of course."

I rolled my eyes. What did she mean, *of course*? Who but my mom would think it would be normal to bring a robot to school?

"Every day?" I asked her.

"You bet. Just like any other kid," Mom answered. "But you can't tell anyone he's a robot. He's part of a secret project I'm working on."

"Secret project?" I asked.

"Java is a special kind of robot called an android," Mom explained. "He looks human. He sounds human. He's just like a regular kid, except smarter and stronger."

Suddenly, Java opened his mouth. "Good morning," he said.

Java's voice sounded like a normal eight-year-old kid's. And he looked like a normal eight-year-old kid, too. Maybe this could work. Except for one thing.

Mom's inventions never worked the way they were supposed to.

"I can't do this," I said. "Can you imagine how the other kids at school will tease me if they find out I have a robot cousin?"

"No one will know." Mom smiled. "He's like any other kid. What could go wrong?"

"Are you kidding? Do you remember the dancing teddy bear you made me in first grade?

I brought him for show-and-tell. He
went crazy! He stuck his finger up Mrs.
Slater's nose. And I couldn't get him to
turn off."

"That was a small
problem," Mom
said. "I fixed it
later."

"Mrs. Slater
never
forgave me,"
I mumbled.
Java stuck
his finger up
his nose. "This is not such a nice feeling,"
he said. "I do not blame her."

"Java is different," Mom promised. "I've been working on him for months. Nothing will go wrong this time. You'll see."

Mom started to walk out of the garage and toward the house. Java stood up and followed her. He walked like a regular kid. There was nothing robot-like about him.

"Java has the brain of a computer," Mom told me. "So he can help you with some of those tough math problems. And it will be nice to have someone around to help with your chores."

That actually sounded pretty good.

As we walked back into the kitchen, Mom frowned. "It's a pigsty in here," she said.

Java looked around. "I do not see any animals."

"Is he for real?" I groaned.

"Almost," Mom said with a laugh.

Almost wasn't good enough. I couldn't take Java to school. It was too weird. I had to get out of it.

Aachoooo! I let

out a fake sneeze.

"I can't go to school," I told Mom. "I think I caught a bug. I better stay home."

"I can do it!" Java shouted, as a fly whizzed by under his nose. He clapped his hands together, trapping the fly in midair.

"I caught a bug, too," he said. "But why would that keep me home from school?"

I looked at Mom nervously. Java didn't act like a normal kid at all.

"He doesn't always understand," Mom admitted. "But the more he's around real kids, the more humanlike he'll learn to be. It's going to be okay. You're just getting cold feet."

I knew that meant I was nervous.

"I'll say," I told Mom. "How do you cure cold feet when you're worried about something like a robot cousin ruining your life?"

"I can do it!" Java shouted. He jumped up, grabbed a blanket from the living-room couch, and laid it over my sneakers.

"What are you doing?" I asked him.

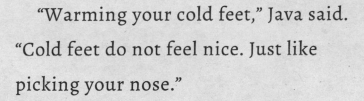

"Warming your cold feet," Java said. "Cold feet do not feel nice. Just like picking your nose."

"Boys, you'd better hurry," Mom told us. "The bus will be here any minute. And remember, Logan. No one can know Java is a robot. It has to be our secret."

I looked at the stunned fly on the counter and the blanket on my feet. Keeping Java's true identity a secret was *not* going to be easy.

3.

Just Act Normal

"Please act like a normal kid," I begged
Java as we walked to the bus stop.

"I will," Java answered. "I am
programmed to act like a normal kid."

Oh, brother.

"Hey, Logan!" my best friend, Stanley,
called to me from the stop. He was
wearing a T-shirt with a hunk of Swiss

cheese on it that said, Say Cheese and Mean It.

"Hi, Stanley," I said. "What's new?"

Stanley shrugged. "Same old stuff." He looked at Java. "Who are you?"

"I am Java!" he said loudly. "Logan is my cousin." Java held out his hand to shake. Stanley stared at him.

Leave it to my mom to program a robot with perfect manners.

"Java's staying with us while his parents are delivering pancakes to hungry rhinos in Transylvania," I said quickly.

Then I caught myself. I didn't even know if rhinos came from

Transylvania. Or if they ate pancakes.

Luckily, neither did Stanley. He just said, "Oh."

"He's finishing the school year here, with us," I continued.

"Cool," Stanley said. He looked behind me to see if the bus was coming. "Hey," he whispered. "Here she comes."

Java turned to see who was coming. His head spun really far— almost the whole way around.

"Whoa!" Stanley exclaimed. "How did you do that?"

"Yoga," I said before Java could answer. "It makes him really stretchy."

"The person coming up behind you is a girl with curly brown hair," Java told me.

"I know," I said. "That's Nadine Vardez." I clutched my stomach.

"Are you in pain?" Java asked.

I shook my head. "No. It's just that every time Nadine comes near me I get butterflies in my stomach. I wish I could get rid of that feeling."

"I can do it!" Java shouted.

Suddenly, Java grabbed me and lifted me over his head. He flipped me over and started shaking me up and down.

Stanley stood there, staring. He couldn't believe it.

Neither could I. "Wha . . . what . . . are y . . . you . . . do . . . doing?!" My voice came out all wobbly.

"I am trying to shake the butterflies out of your stomach." Java peered into my mouth. "They must be stuck down there."

"Put me down!" I ordered.

"Okay." Java flipped me over and dropped me right on my rear end. *In front of Nadine Vardez.*

Quickly, I scrambled to my feet.

"Hi, Logan," Nadine said. "Who's your super-strong friend?"

"He's my cousin. His name is Java."

"Cool name." Nadine smiled right at him.

That didn't seem to make Java nervous at all. I guess robots don't get nervous.

Just then, the bus pulled up, and we all climbed onboard. Java took a seat by a window. I tried to sit next to him, but Nadine beat me to it.

"Where are you from, Java?" Nadine asked.

"Logan's garage," Java answered. "That is where the lab is."

"He means he's staying in my garage for now," I said quickly. "My mom is having a room made for him in there. He's actually from some place . . . um . . . far away."

Nadine opened her mouth to ask another question. But I didn't think I could make up any more answers. So I changed the subject.

"Do you and Cayla have any ideas for your science fair project?" I asked.

"We came up with our idea last night," Nadine said. "We had to. The science fair is next week."

"What is a science fair?" Java asked.

"Didn't they have one in your old school?" she asked him.

"Java used to be homeschooled," I told her. It wasn't a lie, exactly. My Mom *did* program Java at home.

"The science fair is a huge deal," Nadine explained. "Everyone brings in science projects. The best project for every grade wins a prize."

"Have *you* won a prize, Logan?" Java asked me.

Suddenly I heard laughter coming from the seat in front of me. Up popped the Silverspoon twins, wearing their usual matching sweaters.

"Logan's never won anything—" Sherry Silverspoon said.

"—because we always win—" Jerry Silverspoon added.

"—everything!" the twins said at the same time.

"Oh, yeah?" I shouted back at them. "This year, Stanley and I are working together. We're going to do something amazing."

"Is it going to be as big a disaster as your magic trick at the talent show?" Jerry asked.

"When you tried to pull a rabbit out of your hat, and it wasn't there?" Sherry added.

The twins started to laugh.

"It's not my fault the rabbit ran away!" I told them. "Besides, this will be different. Our invention is going to knock it out of the park."

"That is a baseball term," Java said. "Is the science fair at a baseball stadium?"

The twins laughed and turned back

around in their seats. But as the bus
pulled up to school, I heard them
whispering:

"There's something weird about that
new kid," Sherry said.

"Yeah," Jerry agreed. "And *we're* going
to find out what it is."

4.

Trouble Times Two

"Miss Perriwinkle, this is my cousin Java," I said as my robot cousin and I walked up to the teacher's desk. "He's new."

Miss Perriwinkle smiled. "Hello Java," she said. "I'm happy to meet you. Logan's mother has told me all about you."

Not all, I thought to myself. *There are a few nuts and bolts Mom probably didn't mention.*

"We have an extra desk in the front row," Miss Perriwinkle told Java. "Please take that seat."

"**I can do it!**" Java shouted.

He walked over to the desk and picked up the chair.

"What are you doing?" Miss Perriwinkle asked him. She sounded surprised.

I didn't blame her.

"You said to take this seat," Java replied. "Where would you like me to take it?"

The kids all started to laugh. *Except me.*

"Java, put the chair back behind the desk," Miss Perriwinkle said sternly. "And sit on it."

Java did exactly as he was told.

"Class, pull out your math workbooks," Miss Perriwinkle told us. "Let's try the problem on page forty-seven. How much is eight hundred seventy-nine divided by three?"

The Silverspoon twins' hands shot up in the air. *Those two always think they're math geniuses.*

Miss Perriwinkle pointed toward Jerry. But before she could call on him . . .

"Two hundred ninety-three," Java shouted out.

"That's correct, Java." Miss Perriwinkle looked down at his workbook. There was nothing written in it. "Did you just figure that out in your head?" she asked, surprised.

"Actually, my hard drive is in my stomach," Java explained.

Uh-oh.

"He means he had a good breakfast, so he's able to do his best work," I said quickly.

"Java called out the answer!" Jerry Silverspoon tattled to the teacher.

"That's true," Miss Perriwinkle said. "Java, in this class, we raise our hands before we answer a question."

The Silverspoon twins smiled smugly.

"Java, would you like to try another math problem?" Miss Perriwinkle asked.

"Yes," Java replied.

"Okay, what is four thousand two hundred seven times four?" she asked.

I saw the Silverspoon twins write down the problem. They were trying to solve it before Java could. But the Silverspoons do not have calculators in their bellies.

"Sixteen thousand eight hundred twenty-eight," Java said, before the twins could even begin to multiply.

"That's correct!" Miss Perriwinkle said. She looked thrilled to have a math whiz in her class.

The Silverspoon twins glared at Java. They were not happy.

But I was. It was nice to see someone show up those two show-offs for a change.

The Silverspoon twins started whispering back and forth. I had a feeling they were planning something. I didn't know what it was.

But I was pretty sure it wasn't going to be good for Java.

5.

Ready for Takeoff!

"Come on, Stanley," I whined at recess that afternoon. "Just pick a card. One more card. That's all I'm asking."

Stanley looked at my deck of magic playing cards, the one with the superheroes on the back. "But you always get that trick wrong," he said. "I don't want to do it again."

I frowned and put the cards back in my pocket.

"That is an easy trick," Java said. "All you have to do is . . ."

I put my hand over his metallic mouth. A magician never gives away his secrets. And neither does his robot cousin.

"Java! Come play tetherball with us!" the Silverspoon twins called from across the playground.

Java started to walk toward them. But I jumped in front of him.

"Where do you think you're going?"

"To play tetherball with my new friends," Java replied.

"The Silverspoons are your friends?" I asked. "They're not friends with anybody."

"Why not?" Java asked.

I didn't have an answer for that.

I looked at Stanley. He didn't have an answer either.

So I had to let Java go.

"You're not going to send your cousin over to the Silverspoon twins alone are you?" Stanley asked me.

He was right. There was no way Java should be alone with the twins. They were too dangerous. So I followed him to the tetherball pole.

"What are you doing here?" Sherry Silverspoon asked me.

"We only invited Java," Jerry Silverspoon added.

"Java and I are a team. It's us against you guys."

"That's fine," Jerry said. "We'll still beat you."

"We can win a tetherball game with our eyes closed," Sherry bragged.

"**I can do it!**" Java shouted.

He shut his eyes tight and swung his arms wildly, searching for the ball. Java's arms moved so hard and so fast that a wind began to blow. It felt like a hurricane.

Whoosh! The ball whizzed around the pole.

Sherry reached for it, but it was spinning too fast for her.

Jerry jumped up and tried to slam it. But he couldn't.

Humans are no match for robots!

The rope spun faster and faster, winding itself around and around the pole. It moved so hard and so fast it pulled the pole right out of the ground.

The pole shot up into the sky like a helicopter! And the rope was completely wrapped around it. Which meant . . .

"We win!" I exclaimed.

"I can win with my eyes closed, too!"
Java said.

The Silverspoon twins stared at him,
their mouths wide open.

"You're one weird kid," Jerry said.

"But you're a winner," Sherry added.

"We like winners," they said together.

"You should be in our group for the science fair," Jerry said.

So *that* was their plan. They were going to trick my super-smart cousin into working on their science project with them by pretending to be his friends.

It wasn't fair. Java was *my* android. I wanted him to use his super-smart computer brain to help Stanley and me with our science project.

We wanted to make something really cool—something that could move or light up. Not like last year's tornado in a bottle. Four other groups had done the same thing.

It wasn't going to be easy to come up with a project that could win first prize. But three heads would be better than one. Especially if one of them was a super-smart robot head.

The Silverspoon twins had to be stopped!

6.

Top Secret

"You're not going to believe what the Silverspoon twins did to me!" I called out as I ran into Mom's lab after school.

Mom flipped up her goggles and turned off her fiery torch.

"What did they do now, honey?" she asked.

"They tricked Java into helping them with their science fair project!" I  answered. "It's just like them to do something like that."

"How did they trick him?" Mom wondered.

"They asked him," I replied. "And he didn't know he was supposed to say no."

"Why should he say no?" Mom asked.

"Because he's *my* android," I whined.

"He may be part of our family," Mom agreed, "but he's programmed to be his own person. He needs to act like a real kid."

"Real kids are *not* friends with the Silverspoons," I grumbled.

Mom looked around. "Where is Java now?"

"In the living room with *them*." I couldn't believe Mom wasn't taking my side. "Stanley's in the house, too, waiting for me."

"Then don't you think you should go in the house?" Mom asked.

She was right. It wasn't fair to leave my best friend alone with those twins.

Of course, if it wasn't for *her* robot, the Silverspoons wouldn't even be in our house. And they wouldn't have a super-smart robot helping them with their project.

But I wasn't going to let any of that stop me. In fact, I was going to make it impossible for the Silverspoons and Java to win first prize.

I grabbed all the copper wires, a hammer, and a whole box of nails from Mom's toolbox. That was more than Stanley and I would need for our project, but I wanted to make sure the Silverspoons couldn't get their hands on my mom's supplies.

They already had our robot.

"Wait for me," Mom said. "I want to observe Java with his new friends."

I wished she'd stop calling the twins his *friends*.

The first thing I saw when I came back into the house was Stanley's butt sticking out of the pantry.

"What are you looking for, Stanley?" Mom asked.

"The materials for our science fair project," Stanley said.

"*Shhh* . . . the project's a secret," I reminded him.

Just then, the Silverspoon twins and Java walked into the kitchen. I hid the wires behind my back. Stanley closed the pantry door.

"Good afternoon, Mrs. Applebaum," Sherry said.

"So nice to see you," Jerry added.

Mom smiled at the twins.

I couldn't believe she was falling for their nice-kid act.

Mom went into the refrigerator and pulled out five cans of soda. "Anyone want a soft drink?"

I wanted a soda. But I didn't want to put the nails and wires down to open it. That might give away our secret project.

"Hey, Stanley," I asked. "Open one of those for me, will ya?"

"**I can do it!**" Java shouted. He grabbed a can and squeezed. The can popped open in his fist. Fizzy brown cola exploded all over the kitchen.

Boy, was he strong.

"This canned drink is not *soft*," Java told my mom. "It is hard, actually."

The Silverspoon twins stared at Java. Their eyes nearly popped out of their heads.

"Java, quit kidding around." I nudged him with my elbow.

Java looked at me. He had no idea what I was talking about.

"You kids should probably get to work," Mom said as she wiped up spilled cola from the floor.

"We're using the kitchen," I told Java and the Silverspoons. "You guys can work in the living room."

As Java and the twins walked away, Stanley started laughing. "Your cousin's hilarious."

I rolled my eyes. "Yeah. A real riot."

Stanley went back to the pantry and pulled out a big bag of potatoes. "We'll need one of these to make the electric battery," he said.

"I don't get it. Are potatoes electric?"

"No," Stanley told me. "The nails and the wires work together inside the potato to make heat energy. Then the energy is forced into the clock."

He held up the small electric clock we were going to attach to our battery.

"You're *sure* a potato battery will be powerful enough to turn on the clock?" I asked.

Stanley nodded. "That's what it said in the book."

It was a good thing Stanley had found a science book with all the instructions for our project. I had been so busy trying to master my disappearing scarf trick, I had kind of forgotten about it.

"The first thing we have to do is hammer a nail into the potato," Stanley told me.

"Okay." I started hammering.

Splat! The potato broke into a billion pieces that scattered all over the room.

I pulled out another potato and started hammering.

By the time I was on my seventh potato, I heard laughter coming from behind the kitchen door. I walked over and slammed the door shut.

Bam! It hit Jerry right in the nose.

"Quit spying on us!" I yelled at the twins.

"We're not spying!" Sherry giggled.

But I knew they were. And I knew they had seen the potato and the wires. I shot Stanley a look.

The Silverspoon twins were on to us.

7.

Splash Attack!

"I can't believe you're spying on your own cousin," Stanley said to me a little while later.

"I'm not," I insisted. "I'm spying on those nosy Silverspoons. Java just *happens* to be in the living room with them."

I opened the door to the living room just a crack. That's when I heard giggling.

"What's the big deal, Java?" I heard Sherry ask.

"It's just a balloon," Jerry added. "I had it in my pocket. I filled it with water when I went to the bathroom."

"But water will destroy the potato battery Logan and Stanley just made," I overheard Java say.

"Duh," Jerry said.

"That's the point," Sherry added.

I hurried back to the kitchen.

"Uh-oh, Stanley. They're going to give our battery a bath!"

"That will ruin everything," Stanley said. "We have to stop them."

But there wasn't time. The next thing I knew, the Silverspoon twins were in the kitchen. Jerry was holding a big, purple water balloon in his hands.

Java ran past them. He threw himself over our potato.

Wow! My cousin tried to protect my project.

But the twins didn't care.

Jerry held up the water balloon. It looked like he was going to throw it at Java's head!

I couldn't let that happen. There was no telling what water might do to Java's electrical system.

Jerry let the water balloon fly. I leaped up and caught it in midair!

Splat!

The balloon burst in my arms. Water splattered all over my face—and the kitchen counter.

Another mess.
Boy, was Mom
gonna be mad.

"It wasn't my
fault," I told Mom a
little while later as she
finished making dinner. "That water was
going to get all over Java. I freaked out. I
guess I lost my head."

"**I can do it!**" Java shouted suddenly.
He reached up and unscrewed his head
from his body.

I looked over at my headless cousin.

That was actually a
pretty neat trick. And
yet . . .

"That's cool," I told Java.
"Just don't do it in school, okay?"

"Sure," Java's head said.

Java reached up and screwed
his head back onto his neck.

"Thanks for saving our
potato project. That was a lot of hard
work. I wouldn't want to have to do it all
over again," I told him.

"Dinner time!" Mom said. She plopped
a platter of hamburgers and mashed
potatoes on the table.

I scooped up a pile of potatoes and

began stuffing my face.

"I sure do love mashed potatoes," I said between spoonfuls. "You hardly ever make them."

"That's because the potatoes take so long to boil," Mom answered. "But I thought you deserved a reward for being so nice to Java. It can't be easy."

No kidding.

"You actually have the twins to thank for those potatoes," Mom continued. "It was their idea."

I shoved another spoonful into my mouth and . . . pulled out a long copper wire!

"You mashed up my science project!" I
yelled.

Mom stared at me. "I'm sorry. The
potato was just sitting there on the table.
The twins said that's where they got the
idea for dinner."

I frowned. Our project was ruined.
Now Stanley and I were going to have to
start all over again.

The Silverspoon
twins had done it
to me again.

8.

No Lava for Java

"Stanley, can you stop reading and help?"
I asked as I nudged my science fair
partner in the arm.

Instead of working on setting up
our display in the school gym, he was
studying a book about birdcalls.

"I don't know why you always have
your nose in a book," I said to him.

"I like reading," Stanley said.

"**I can do it!**" Java announced loudly. He yanked the book from Stanley's hands and stuck his nose between the pages.

"I do not understand how Stanley can read with his nose in a book," Java said. "Can he see through his nostrils?"

Stanley glared at Java and grabbed back his book.

"Java, go set up your own project," I insisted.

I didn't want my cousin doing anything else embarrassing.

Especially not when Nadine and her partner, Cayla, were setting up their project right next to our Supersonic Spud Machine—otherwise known as our potato battery.

Nadine and Cayla's project showed how magnets could be used to move metal. They had drawn a face on a piece of cardboard. There were metal chips all around the head.

Cayla was using a huge magnet to move the metal chips around the face. *Ha! That metal mustache looked really funny.*

Their magnet project was pretty cool. But not as cool as our potato battery. We still had a chance to win first prize.

I looked around the room to check out the rest of the competition. Kids were pouring candies into cola bottles as their parents waited excitedly for explosions.

There were also about a gazillion volcanoes with fake, erupting lava. Every time one went off, a group of parents cheered.

Those were pretty simple experiments.
Not like our Supersonic Spud Machine.
Ours was a much more grown-up kind
of project. Stanley and I weren't making
anything explode.

There was no lava for Java, either. He
and the Silverspoons had built a beehive.
With *real, live* buzzing bees.

Jerry and Sherry were standing by
their table, trying to get people to come
admire their honeybees. They were
wearing matching white beekeeper suits
that made them look like space cadets.

Java stood near them, in his school
clothes, spouting bee facts to anyone
who happened to pass by their table.

"Bees live on every continent except Antarctica. There are three kinds of bees in a hive: the queen bee, the worker bees, and the drones . . ."

Just then, I saw Nadine go over and pull Java by the arm.

"Hey, Java. Come try out our magnet project," she said as she held up a giant magnet. "It would be funny if you gave him a twisty beard."

I frowned. Nadine hadn't asked me to make a twisty beard. She hadn't asked *me* to make anything.

"KO!" Java shouted.

"Don't you mean okay?" Nadine asked him.

"The average person spends three years sitting on the toilet," he replied.

Nadine gave him a funny look. "What are you talking about?"

"The world's stinkiest cheese comes from France." Java bent over and started reaching for his rear end. He spun around in a circle.

He looked like a dog chasing his tail.

Then he started *barking* like a dog. *"Ruff. Ruff. Woof. W—"*

Java stopped mid woof. He stood there staring into space.

Phew. I was glad that was over.

"Cows can go up stairs, but they can't come down again," Java blurted out suddenly. *"Moo, Moo!"*

But it *wasn't* over. *Why was my cousin acting so weird?*

A group of kids gathered around. They stared at him.

"A blue whale's head is so big that fifty football players could stand on its tongue." Java started talking faster and faster. "Hairy spiders make milk. Cats cannot taste sweets. The longest toenail is . . ."

Suddenly, smoke blasted out of Java's ears, nose, and mouth. Steam exploded from his rear end.

Something was really, really wrong.

9.

What's the Buzz?

"MOM!" I shouted. "HELP!"

My mom came running over.

"Look at him," I said, pointing to Java. "He's exploding!"

Blasts of green, yellow, and red lights were shooting out from Java's eyes. They looked like stoplights.

"Do something, Mom! People are staring."

"There's a lot of metal inside Java," she said. "Nadine's magnet must be moving it around. We have to get him into a quiet room where I can rewire him."

"I'll get him!" I shouted.

I ran over and grabbed my android cousin by the arm. I tried to drag him from the gym.

But Java was too strong to be dragged by a human boy. He yanked himself free and started spinning around on his head.

What was I going to do now?

I looked at the giant magnet in Nadine's hand and . . . suddenly I had a fantastic idea!

I grabbed the second magnet from Nadine and Cayla's project. Hopefully, my magnet would pull Java right toward me. Then I could drag him away from everybody else.

I held up the magnet. Java started moving in my direction.

"I can do it! I can do it! I can do it!" Java shouted over and over.

Uh-oh. There was no telling what could happen when Java said that. I had to get him out of there.

"I thought you wanted to try my project!" Nadine said to Java. She held up her magnet and tried to hand it to him.

Java started being pulled toward Nadine.

I couldn't let that happen.

I held my magnet closer to Java. He moved toward me again.

Nadine moved her magnet closer to Java. He pulled toward her.

Now, it was tug-of-war. And I couldn't let Nadine win. I moved my magnet even closer.

Java slid between the magnets. Back and forth.

Back and forth.

Back and . . .

CRASH!

Java tripped over his shoelace and slammed into the Silverspoons!

The twins fell right into their beehive.

It smashed on the floor.

Everyone turned and stared.

A honeybee flew out of the hive and started to circle around the gym.

Another bee followed him.

And another.

Then suddenly . . .

Buzzzzzzzzzzz.

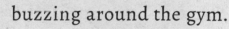

It seemed like about a billion bees broke out of the hive! They started

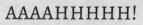

buzzing around the gym.

AAAAHHHHH!

Everyone was screaming! People stampeded out of the room. They couldn't get away from the angry

insects fast enough.

Kaboom!

Suddenly, Principal Kumquat knocked over a volcano. Ooey-gooey lava erupted and spilled all over the floor.

Whoosh!

Teachers, students, and parents all started slipping and sliding through the gooey gunk as they raced toward the door.

Crash!

Smash!

Everyone looked like human bumper cars as they hurried to get out of the way of the zooming army of Silverspoon bees!

The twins were running around and around in circles. Jerry was holding the

hive. Sherry was trying to catch bees in a glass jar.

Slam!

Jerry smacked right into Sherry. Sticky, yellow honey dripped from the hive. The twins stuck together like glued paper!

Now, that was funny!

Ha-ha-ha . . . "Ouch!" I cried as one of the bees stung me right in the butt. Boy, did that hurt.

I looked over at my robot cousin. Bees were zooming at him from all sides. But he wasn't crying. He wasn't even hurt.

Bee stings can't do anything to robots.

It's magnets that mess *them* up.

10.

Time's Up!

"That might have been the strangest science fair we've ever had," Stanley said as we stood outside school the next morning.

"You're telling me," I agreed. "These bee stings on my butt hurt! I don't think I'll be able to sit down for a week."

"The judges didn't even get a chance to give prizes for the best projects," Stanley said.

"At least the Silverspoon twins didn't win," I said. "That's something."

I looked over by the flagpole. Java was standing there all by himself. I felt bad for him. But I didn't want to be around him right then, either.

He wasn't alone for long. The Silverspoon twins were stomping over to him.

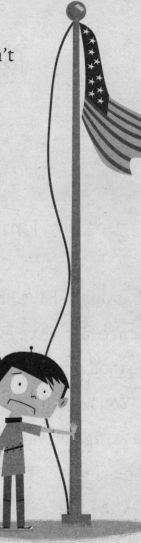

"You ruined our project!" Sherry shouted.

"And the whole science fair," Jerry added.

"You freak," the twins said at the same time.

That did it!

I hurried over to the flagpole to rescue my cousin from the evil twins.

"Who are you calling a freak?" I asked.

"You and your weirdo cousin, Java," Sherry said.

"You can't talk that way to my family!" I shouted.

Then I stopped. I couldn't believe I was calling a bucket of bolts "my family."

But that's what it felt like.

The twins glared at Java and me.

"You're going to be sorry you kept us from winning," Sherry said.

"You'd better watch out," Jerry added. "No one messes with the Silverspoon twins!"

They rolled their eyes and walked away.

A moment later, Nadine came over. "Java, you were hilarious yesterday!" She giggled. "Where did you get all those weird facts?"

"The facts are in my hard drive . . ." Java began.

Ha-ha-ha. I laughed over him, loudly. "That's my cousin. He's always full of weird facts." I smiled at Nadine. "So, did you get any bad bee stings yesterday?"

"Not as many as Java got, I'm sure," Nadine said. She smiled at him. "I couldn't believe how brave you were with those bees. You didn't even cry when they stung you, like everyone else did. It's like you're part machine."

Gulp.

"Well, another science fair has come and gone," I said, changing the subject quickly. "It went so fast. Time really flies."

Java looked at me and smiled. "**I can do it!**" he exclaimed as he grabbed my wrist and yanked off my brand-new glow-in-the-dark digital watch.

He threw it way up in the air, higher than the flagpole.

Kablam!

Crack!

My watch plopped down from the sky
and crashed right onto a rock.

"You are incorrect, Logan," Java said.
"Time does not fly."

Nadine burst out laughing. But I didn't think it was so funny.

Brrringgg. The bell rang. It was time to go to class. It was being held on the playground, since the school was still infested with bees.

As I walked toward the slide, I glanced at my cousin. He sure had made things different around here for me. But some things hadn't changed at all.

Stanley was still my best friend.

The Silverspoon twins were still bullies.

Nadine still had no idea that I liked her.

And, luckily, none of them had figured out why Java always acted so strangely. His secret was safe.

For now, anyway.

You can make
Logan and Stanley's

Supersonic Spud Machine!

Turn the page to see how...

Here's what you will need:

- 1 adult to help you make your Supersonic Spud Machine
- 2 medium-sized raw potatoes
- 2 pennies
- 2 zinc (galvanized) nails
- 3 insulated wires each cut to measure 6 to 9 inches long. Ask your adult to strip off two inches of the insulation from one end of each wire.
- 1 hammer
- 1 low-current LED clock

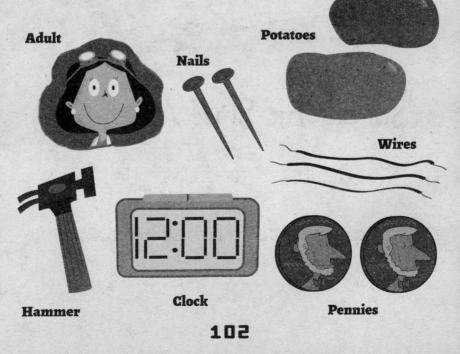

Adult

Nails

Potatoes

Wires

Hammer

Clock

Pennies

Here's what you do:

1 Place the two potatoes on a flat surface.

2 Wrap the end of one piece of wire around one of the nails.

3 Wrap the end of another piece of wire around one of the pennies.

4 Gently hammer the nail and the penny into the first potato. Be careful to make sure that they do not touch each other. (You might want your adult to help with this, too.)

5 Wrap a third piece of wire around the second penny and gently hammer it into the second potato.

6 Gently hammer the other nail into the second potato. Make sure this nail *does not* have any wire wrapped around it.

103

7 Connect the wire from the penny on the first potato to the nail that is stuck into the second potato. (The nail with no wire wrapped around it.)

8 Touch the free ends of the wires in the potatoes to the plus and minus terminals in the battery compartment on the back of your clock.

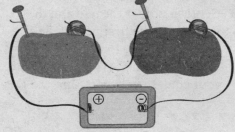

You may have to try connecting the wires to the clock a few different ways, until you get the energy to flow from the potato battery to the clock. But before you know it, your clock will be telling time!

About the Authors

Nancy Krulik is the author of more than two hundred books for children and young adults including three *New York Times* bestsellers and the popular Katie Kazoo, Switcheroo; George Brown, Class Clown; and Magic Bone series. She lives in New York City with her husband and crazy beagle mix.

Amanda Burwasser holds a BFA with honors in creative writing from Pratt Institute in New York City. Her senior thesis earned her the coveted Pratt Circle Award. A preschool teacher, she resides in Santa Rosa, California.

About the Illustrator

Mike Moran is a dad, husband, and illustrator. His illustrations can be seen in children's books, animation, magazines, games, World Series programs, and more. He lives in Florham Park, New Jersey.